How I Hunted
THE
Little Fellows

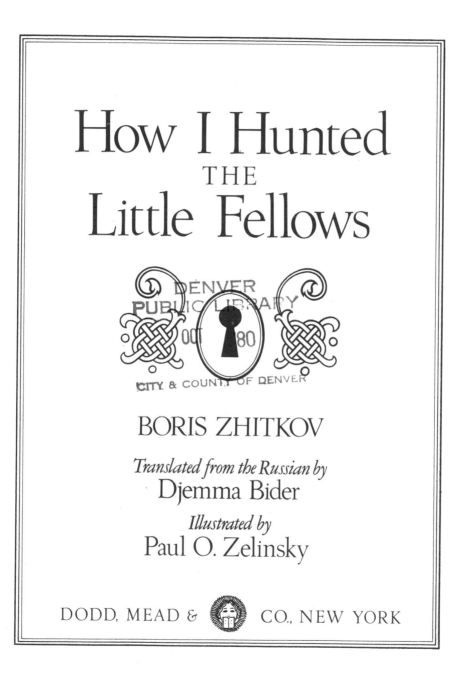

BORIS ZHITKOV

Translated from the Russian by
Djemma Bider

Illustrated by
Paul O. Zelinsky

DODD, MEAD & CO., NEW YORK

1   2   3   4   5   6   7   8   9   10

Library of Congress Cataloging in Publication Data

Zhitkov, Boris Stepanovich, 1882–1938.
How I hunted the little fellows.
SUMMARY: Fascinated by the life-like miniature of
a steamer on his grandmother's shelf, a young boy
becomes convinced that there are little people inside
and, ignoring the admonition not to touch, decides
to find out for himself.
[1. Russia—Fiction]   I. Zelinsky, Paul O.
II. Title.
PZ7.Z48Ho   [Fic]   79-11738
ISBN 0-396-07602-0

JFIC
Z
5
ho

How I Hunted the Little Fellows

WHEN I was a little boy I was taken to stay with my Grandmother for a few weeks. Over the table at Grandmother's house was a shelf, and on the shelf was a small steamship.

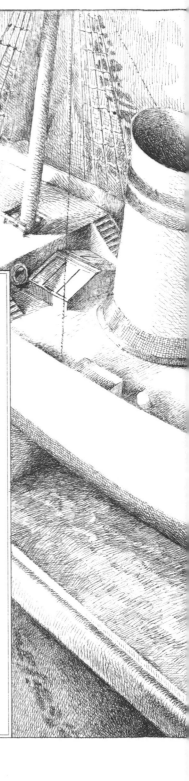

Never in my life had I seen anything like it. Though miniature, it looked absolutely real. It had a yellow smokestack with two black stripes. Its two masts were connected to the sides of the boat by little rope ladders. Aft was a cabin shaped like a small house, polished, with tiny windows and a little door. At the tip of the stern was a copper steering wheel, and below the stern was a rudder. In front of the rudder, the propeller shone like a small copper rose. On the bow were two anchors—wonderful, wonderful anchors. How I wished I could have had even one such anchor!

Right away I asked Grandmother if I might play with the little steamer. She never said no to me, but this time suddenly she frowned.

"That, really, you must not ask. Not only are you not to play with it—don't even dare touch it. Never! It's a dear memory to me."

I understood immediately that even tears wouldn't help me here.

But the little steamship stood proudly

on its polished shelf. I couldn't take my
eyes off it.

"Give your word of honor that you
won't touch it," Grandmother said. "Or
perhaps I had better hide it, so you won't
be tempted." She went toward the shelf.

Close to tears, I shouted at the top of
my lungs, "Word of honor, cross my
heart, Granny!" I caught her by the skirt.

She didn't take away the little steamship.

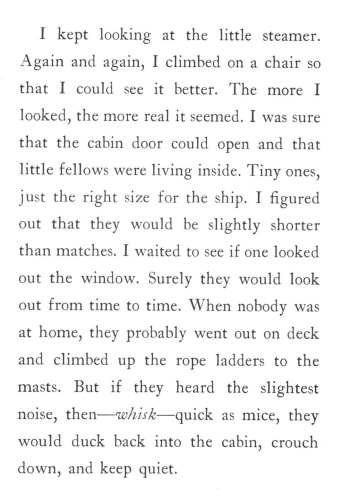

I kept looking at the little steamer. Again and again, I climbed on a chair so that I could see it better. The more I looked, the more real it seemed. I was sure that the cabin door could open and that little fellows were living inside. Tiny ones, just the right size for the ship. I figured out that they would be slightly shorter than matches. I waited to see if one looked out the window. Surely they would look out from time to time. When nobody was at home, they probably went out on deck and climbed up the rope ladders to the masts. But if they heard the slightest noise, then—*whisk*—quick as mice, they would duck back into the cabin, crouch down, and keep quiet.

All afternoon, whenever I was alone in the room, I watched. No one looked out. I hid behind the door and peeked through the keyhole. But the sly little fellows knew that I was spying on them! Aha! So they worked at night, when nobody could see them. Cunning.

That evening I gulped down my tea and asked to go to bed.

"What's all this?" Grandmother said. "Usually I have to force you, and now you ask so early?"

So, we went to bed, and Grandmother put out the light. In the dark, I couldn't see the little steamer. I purposely began to fidget to make the bed creak.

"Why are you tossing and turning so much?" Grandmother asked.

"I'm afraid to sleep without the light. At home they always leave a night-light

burning." This was a lie. At home we kept it dark at night.

Grandmother grumbled a bit, but she got up. She rummaged about and finally arranged a wick in a bowl of lamp oil. It burned badly. Still, in the faint light, I could see the little steamer shining on its shelf.

I pulled the blanket over my head and made a house for myself, leaving a small hole through which I watched without moving a muscle. I soon became used to the dim light and could see everything on the steamer perfectly. I looked at it for a long time. The room was very quiet. Only the clock ticked. Then, suddenly, something rustled. I was all ears. The rustle was coming from the little steamer—it sounded as if the cabin door were opening. I held my breath. Then I inched forward —and the stupid bed creaked! I had frightened off the little fellows!

Now there was nothing to wait for. I fell asleep—out of grief.

The next day, this is what I thought: Surely the little fellows have to eat. One hard candy would seem like a whole cart-load to them. I could crack some candy and put a piece near the cabin door. Just a small piece, but too big to fit through the door easily. At night, the little fellows would peek around the door and see— wow!—a huge piece of candy. Then they'd rush out and start pulling it toward them. They would try to pull it into the cabin, but it wouldn't fit through the door. So they would run and get hatchets— very, very small hatchets, but absolutely real. They would chip away: chop-chop,

chop-chop. Working quickly, to avoid be-ing caught, they would chop and chop and try to push the piece of candy through the door. If the bed happened to creak and if they ran away, still, the candy would be stuck in the door—half in, half out—and I would see how they had dragged it. Maybe in his fright, one of the little fel-lows would drop his hatchet. I would find it lying on the deck, so tiny—but real— and as sharp as could be.

Secretly, so that Grandmother wouldn't see, I broke a piece of hard candy to just the size I wanted. I waited until Grand-mother was busy in the kitchen. Then—

one, two, three—my feet were on the
table, and I put the hard candy right out-
side the cabin door. For the little fellows
it would be just half a step from the door
to the candy.

I climbed down from the table. With
my sleeve I wiped off the dirt that my
shoes had left. Grandmother hadn't
noticed a thing.

I stole a glance at the little steamer whenever I could. Then Grandmother took me for a walk. I was afraid that the little fellows would grab the candy while I was away, and ruin my plans to catch them. So, during the walk, I purposely sniffled and complained that I was cold. Granny took me home early.

The first thing I did was look at the little steamer. The hard candy was right where I had left it! So. They were too smart to risk it during the daytime.

That night, after Grandmother was

asleep, I settled myself in my little blanket house and started to watch. This time the night-light burned perfectly. The hard candy glittered like a piece of ice in the sun. I stared and stared at the shiny spot,

and then—unlucky me—I fell asleep. In the morning I got up early and ran to check, still dressed in my nightshirt. The hard candy was gone. The little fellows had outwitted me after all. Later on I looked again. There was no little hatchet, of course. After all, why should there be? With nobody to bother them, they could have taken their time. Not a single chip of candy was lying around. They had

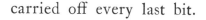

carried off every last bit.

The next time I left bread. That night I heard some commotion, but the stupid night-light hardly glowed, and I could barely make out the little steamer. In the morning, the bread was gone—only a few crumbs remained. Well, now I understood. They didn't care as much for bread—it wasn't sweet. With candy, every last sliver was precious to them.

I couldn't stop thinking about the little fellows. I figured out that inside the little steamer they had benches along both sides. During the day the little fellows sat shoulder to shoulder and whispered quietly to each other. But at night, after everybody in the house was asleep, they began to move about.

I wanted to take a small piece of cloth —for them, a tiny rug—and soak it in ink. I would put it by the cabin door, and when they ran out, they would step in the ink before they realized it was there, and leave footprints all over. Then at least I would see what kind of feet they had.

Maybe some of them went barefoot, to keep from making noise.

But no, they were so clever they would just laugh at all my tricks.

I couldn't stand it any more.

I decided once and for all to take the little steamship down, to look at it, and to catch the little fellows—at least one. I had to find a way to be home alone. Grandmother dragged me everywhere on her visits, always to some old women. They would whisper together for half a day. And I would have to sit and not touch anything. I was only allowed to stroke the cat.

As it happened, Grandmother was getting ready to go out. I saw her putting some biscuits into a little box, to take along for tea. I ran to the hallway, picked up my knitted mittens, and not sparing myself, rubbed my forehead and cheeks, my whole face really, as hard as I could. Then I lay quietly on the bed.

All of a sudden Grandmother missed me. "Boria! Boriushka! Where are you?"

I kept still and closed my eyes. Grand-mother came over to me.

"Why are you lying down?"

"I have a headache."

She touched my forehead.

"Boriushka, listen to me. You stay home. On my way back, I will bring you some dried raspberries from the druggist. I'll be back soon. I won't be gone long. You undress and go to bed. Lie down, lie down. And don't argue!"

She helped me undress, put me to bed, and tucked in the blanket. Over and over she said, "I will be back soon, quick as a wink."

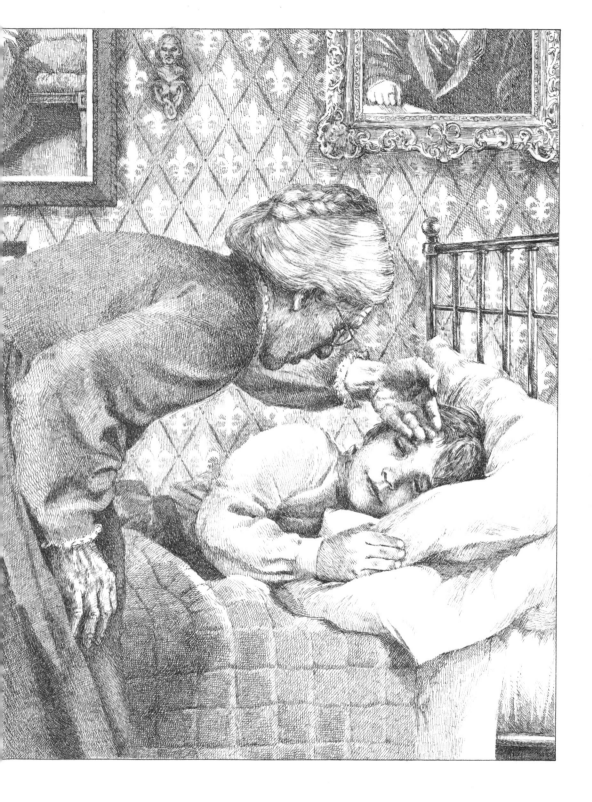

Grandmother locked the door with a key. I waited five minutes. What if she came back? Suppose she had forgotten something?

Then I jumped out of bed. I leaped on the table and took the little steamer from its shelf. I could tell instantly that it was made of iron. A real ship! I pressed it to my ear and listened. Were they moving? They certainly were keeping quiet. They understood that I had captured their ship.

Aha! They were sitting on their benches silent as mice.

I carried the little steamer down from the table and started to shake it. I thought: I will shake the little fellows off their benches. They won't be able to remain sitting, and I shall hear how they scramble around.

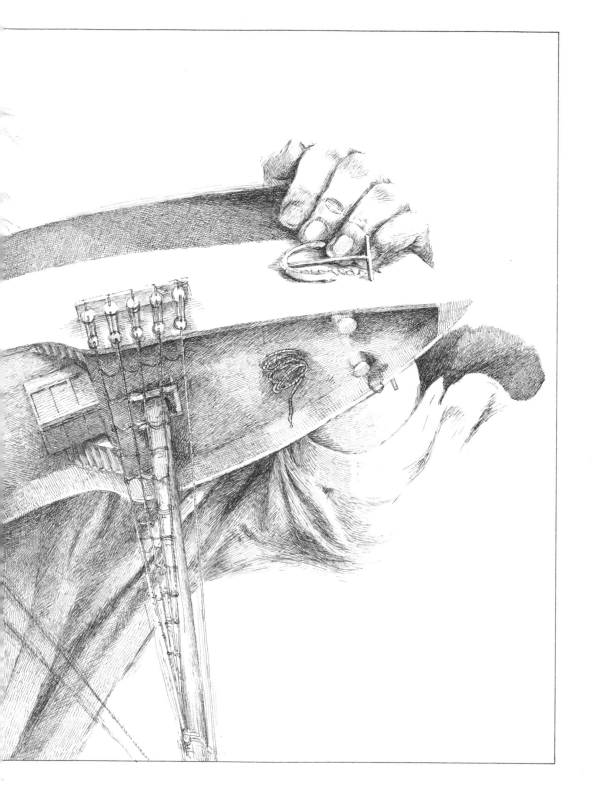

But inside it was quiet. Then I understood. They were sitting side by side on
the benches, tucking their legs in under
the boards and holding on with all their
strength. They sat as if glued to their
seats.

But wait! If I could pry the deck loose,
I would catch them all!

I reached for a knife that was in the sideboard, but didn't take my eyes off the steamer, in case the little fellows tried to leap out. I tried to slip the knife in along the edge of the deck. Ugh! How tight everything was.

At last I managed to push the knife through and wiggle it slightly. The masts

rose with the deck, but the rope ladders held the deck down. I had to cut them; otherwise it wouldn't work. I stopped for a second—only a second. Hurrying, I started to saw the ladders. The knife was blunt, but finally it was done. The ladders hung limp. The masts were free. With the knife, I began to raise the deck again. I was afraid to lift the deck up high, in case the little fellows might jump out and scatter. So I lifted the deck just a crack, so that only one could get through. He would start to climb out, but—*bang!*—I would catch him like a beetle in my palm.

I waited, keeping my hand ready.

No one climbed out. I decided to force the deck up in one big motion and slam my hand down. That way I would get at least one. Only it had to be done fast. They would probably be waiting for me, ready to scatter.

I pulled the deck up and slammed my hand down.

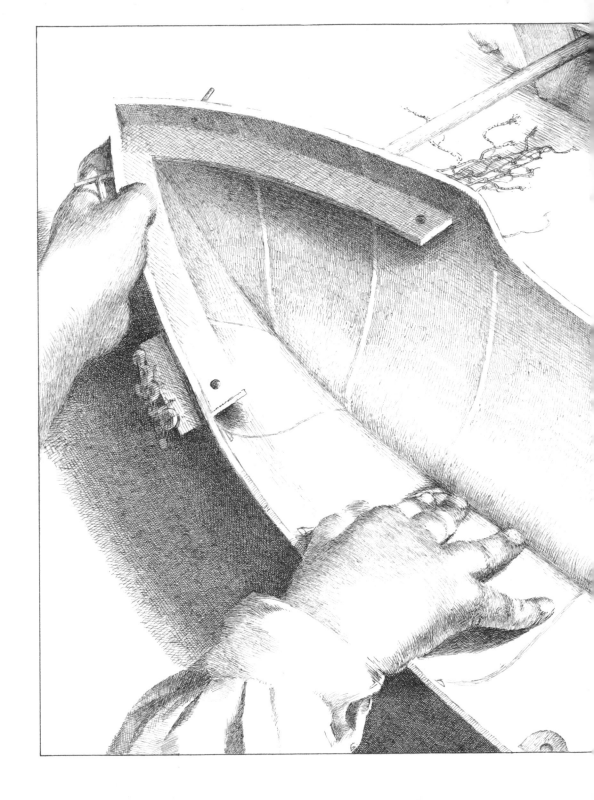

Nothing! Absolutely, absolutely nothing! There weren't even any benches. Nothing but bare, empty sides, like a stewpot. I lifted my hand. Sure enough, there was nothing under it, either.

My fingers shook as I tried to fit the deck back into the hull. It was no good. Everything was bent and stood out crookedly. It was impossible to attach the rope ladders to the sides. They just dangled in the air.

Somehow I stuck the deck in place, climbed on the table, and put the little steamship back on its shelf.

Everything was lost now!

I threw myself into bed and buried

myself under the covers. I heard a key in the door.

"Granny," I whispered under the blanket. "Granny, my dearest own Granny, what have I done!"

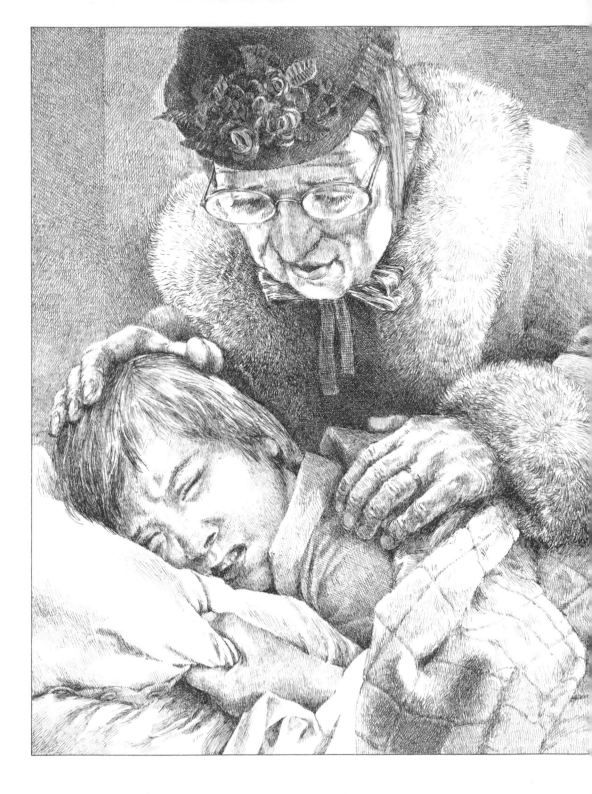

But Grandmother was already standing over me, patting my head.

"Why are you sobbing, Boriushka, why are you weeping? My dearest, my darling, you see how quickly I came back?"

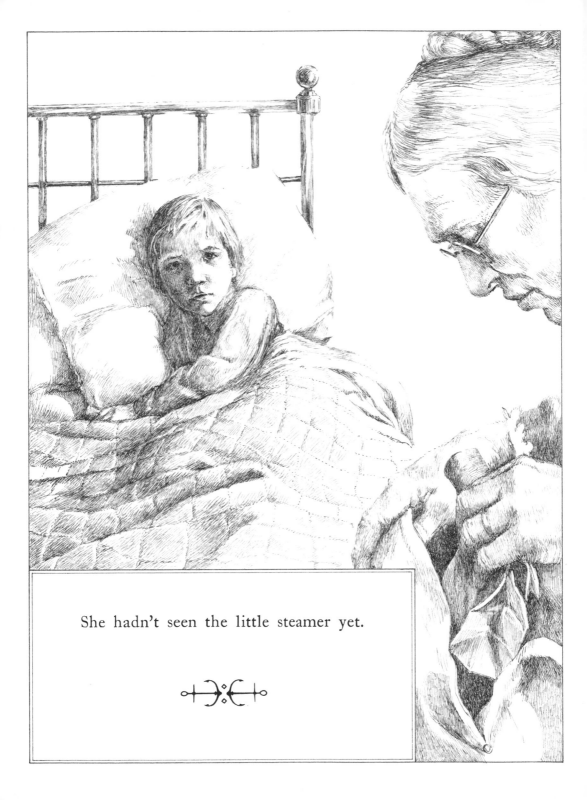

She hadn't seen the little steamer yet.

BORIS ZHITKOV (1882–1938) was born in Novgorod into a cultivated Russian family. His father was a mathematician, his mother a pianist. He had three sisters. When he was eight, his family moved to Odessa, where they lived by the harbor, and the young Boris fell in love with the Black Sea. The sea, ships, and colorful people of all nationalities remained among his chief lifelong interests.

Zhitkov was an immensely versatile man. He was an engineer, a chemist, a mathematician, a shipbuilder. He was knowledgeable in astronomy, botany, and other natural sciences. He sailed every ocean and visited many of the exotic countries that could be reached by sea. An outstanding athlete, a gifted photographer, he played violin, danced, and choreographed two ballets with Nijinsky (who became famous later). He had the ability to absorb all he saw, the gift of remembering everything, and, above all, the power to enthrall listeners with his tales.

His life was by no means easy, however. During the Russian Revolution, he nearly died from starvation. By the end of 1923, he was in Petrograd, jobless and living in dire poverty. Even the cost of a streetcar ticket was a problem.

Tired, sick, and gloomy, he visited Kornei Chukovsky, a well-known writer. While Chukovsky was busy, Zhitkov entertained his children by telling them about his sea adventures. Chukovsky heard his children's obvious delight from the next room. "More! More!" they were shouting.

"How about becoming a writer?" Chukovsky suggested. "Try to put down on paper what you just told my children, and bring me what you have written." Zhitkov did so, and his manuscript was accepted for publication. Subsequent stories about exotic countries, distant voyages, unusual animals, people of all professions, and children of all ages quickly took their place among the best Russian literature for children. *How I Hunted the Little Fellows* was based on an incident from Zhitkov's own life. After the story was published, he wrote a second story about Boria, never published (in fact lost in an editorial office in Leningrad), in which he told how Boria was so distraught over what he had done that he ran away and hid on a river bank, and how his grandmother forgave him.

Zhitkov firmly believed that an eight-year-old mind differed in no fundamental way from an adult mind. People do acquire experience and knowledge, he believed, but no one can be taught to be intelligent, just as no one can be taught to be talented. A child merits the same respect as an adult. He always felt that a story written for a child should be a work of art.

I am happy to share Zhitkov's world with English-speaking children.

—Djemma Bider

DJEMMA BIDER was born in Bessarabia of Russian parents. In her youth she traveled extensively throughout Europe and studied in Paris. She has both written her own stories and translated the stories and poems of others, among them Chekhov and Nabokov, into English. She has also translated I. B. Singer and Saul Bellow into Russian. The mother of two grown daughters, she lives in New York City.

PAUL O. ZELINSKY studied painting at Yale University and Tyler School of Art. After a brief period teaching painting on the West Coast, he moved to New York City to both paint and illustrate. His work has appeared in such publications as *New York* magazine and *The New York Times*, and he is the illustrator of *Emily Upham's Revenge*, a novel. This is his first picture book.